DRAWING DINOSAURS

DRAWING PTERANODON
AND OTHER FLYING DINOSAURS

STEVE BEAUMONT

PowerKiDS
press.

New York

Published in 2010 by The Rosen Publishing Group, Inc.
29 East 21st Street, New York, NY 10010

Copyright © 2010 Arcturus Publishing Ltd

Artwork and text: Steve Beaumont
Editor (Arcturus): Carron Brown
Designer: Steve Flight

Library of Congress Cataloging-in-Publication Data

Beaumont, Steve.
  Drawing Pteranodon and other flying dinosaurs / Steve Beaumont. — 1st ed.
      p. cm. — (Drawing dinosaurs)
  Includes index.
  ISBN 978-1-61531-904-6 (library binding) — ISBN 978-1-4488-0428-3 (pbk.) —
ISBN 978-1-4488-0429-0 (6-pack)
  1. Dinosaurs in art—Juvenile literature. 2. Drawing—Technique—Juvenile literature.
  3. Pteranodon—Juvenile literature. I. Title.
  NC780.5.B3935 2010
  743.6—dc22
                                        2009033318

Printed in China

CPSIA compliance information: Batch #AW0102PK : For further information contact Rosen Publishing, New York, New York at 1-800-237-9932

CONTENTS

"Dinosaurs"… the word conjures up all kinds of powerful and exciting images. The word "dinosaur" is often used to describe all prehistoric reptiles, but not all were true dinosaurs. Pteranodon, Archaeopteryx, and Tropeognathus are flying reptiles and so are not true dinosaurs. One feature that separated the reptiles from the dinosaurs was the structure of their limbs, which were held directly beneath their body. This meant they could stand upright.

These amazing creatures ruled Earth for over 160 million years until, suddenly, they all died out. No one has ever seen a living, moving, roaring dinosaur, but thanks to the research of paleontologists, who piece together dinosaur fossils, we now have a pretty good idea what many of them looked like.

Some were as big as huge buildings, others had enormous teeth, scaly skin, horns, claws, and body armor. Dinosaurs have played starring roles in books, on television, and in blockbuster movies, and now it's time for them to take center stage on your drawing pad!

In this book we've chosen three incredible flying dinosaurs for you to learn how to draw. We've also included an ancient landscape for you to sketch, so you can really set the prehistoric scene for your drawings.

You'll find advice on essential drawing tools, tips on how to get the best results, and easy-to-follow step-by-step instructions showing you how to draw each dinosaur. So, it's time to bring these extinct monsters back to life—let's draw some dinosaurs!

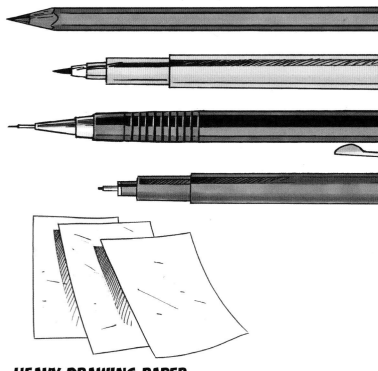

DRAWING TOOLS

Let's start with the essential drawing tools you'll need to create awesome illustrations. Build up your collection as your drawing skills improve.

LAYOUT PAPER

Artists, both as professionals and as students, rarely produce their first practice sketches on their best quality art paper. It's a good idea to buy some inexpensive plain letter-size paper from a stationery store for all of your practice sketches. Buy the least expensive kind.

Most professional illustrators use cheaper paper for basic layouts and practice sketches before they get to the more serious task of producing a masterpiece on more costly material.

HEAVY DRAWING PAPER

This paper is ideal for your final version. You don't have to buy the most expensive brand—most decent arts and crafts stores will stock their own brand or another lower-priced brand and unless you're thinking of turning professional, these will work fine.

WATERCOLOR PAPER

This paper is made from 100 percent cotton and is much higher quality than wood-based papers. Most arts and crafts stores will stock a large range of weights and sizes—140 pounds per ream (300 g/sq m) will be fine.

LINE ART PAPER

If you want to practice black and white ink drawing, line art paper enables you to produce a nice clear crisp line. You'll get better results than you would on heavier paper as it has a much smoother surface.

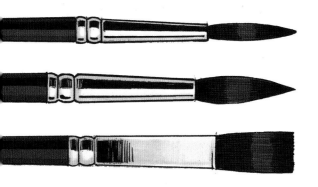

PENCILS

It's best not to cut corners on quality here. Get a good range of graphite (lead) pencils ranging from soft (#1) to hard (#4).

Hard lead lasts longer and leaves less graphite on the paper. Soft lead leaves more lead on the paper and wears down more quickly. Every artist has his personal preference, but #2.5 pencils are a good medium grade to start out with until you find your own favorite.

Spend some time drawing with each grade of pencil and get used to their different qualities. Another good product to try is the clutch, or mechanical pencil. These are available in a range of lead thicknesses, 0.5mm being a good medium size. These pencils are very good for fine detail work.

PENS

There is a large range of good quality pens on the market and all will do a decent job of inking. It's important to experiment with a range of different pens to determine which you find most comfortable to work with.

You may find that you end up using a combination of pens to produce your finished piece of artwork. Remember to use a pen that has waterproof ink if you want to color your illustration with a watercolor or ink wash.

It's a good idea to use one of these—there's nothing worse than having your nicely inked drawing ruined by an accidental drop of water!

BRUSHES

Some artists like to use a fine brush for inking linework. This takes a bit more practice and patience to master, but the results can be very satisfying. If you want to try your hand at brushwork, you will definitely need to get some good-quality sable brushes.

ERASER

There are three main types of erasers: rubber, plastic, and putty. Try all three to see which kind you prefer.

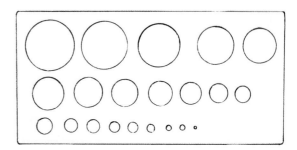

PANTONE MARKERS

These are very versatile pens and with practice can give pleasing results.

INKS

With the rise of computers and digital illustration, materials such as inks have become a bit obscure, so you may have to look harder for these, but most good arts and crafts stores should stock them.

WATERCOLORS AND GOUACHE

Most art stores will stock a wide range of these products, from professional to student quality.

CIRCLE TEMPLATE

This is very useful for drawing small circles.

FRENCH CURVES

These are available in a few shapes and sizes and are useful for drawing curves.

BUILDING DINOSAURS

Notice how a simple oval shape forms the body of these three dinosaurs (figs.1, 2, and 3). Even though they are all very differently shaped, an oval forms the body of each one perfectly.

Fig. 4 shows how a dinosaur can be constructed using all these basic shapes. Cylinders are used for its legs and arms, an oval shape forms its body, and a smaller egg shape is used for its head.

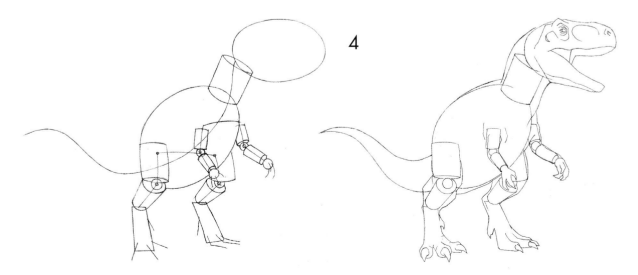

DRAWING DINOSAUR HEADS

The egg shape (fig. 1) can be used as a base to start the heads of most dinosaurs (fig. 2). When it comes to drawing flying reptiles, such as the Pteranodon, an egg shape can still be used with the addition of triangles to form the beak (fig. 3).

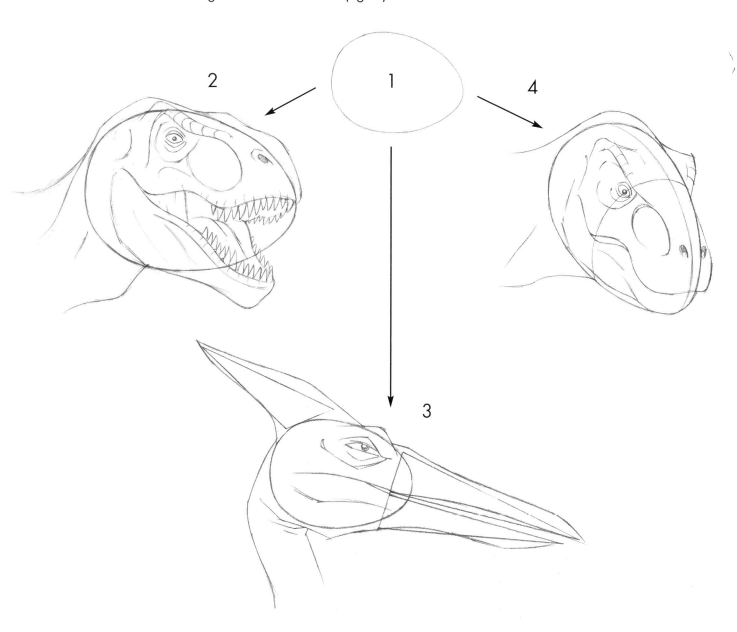

A useful tip when drawing the head of a dinosaur is to divide it up (fig. 4). Start with a central line down the middle and add a horizontal line about a third of the way down to plot where the eyes will sit. This may take a bit of practice, but the more you draw the easier it will become.

PTERANODON

DINO FACT FILE

Pteranodon was a terrifying flying reptile that was as tall as a human, with a massive pair of tough leathery wings. It was an intelligent creature with a big brain and excellent eyesight. Each different species had a unique bony head crest. It was a carnivore and hunted for fish, scooping them up from the water and swallowing them whole since it had no teeth. It also scavenged for dead animals.

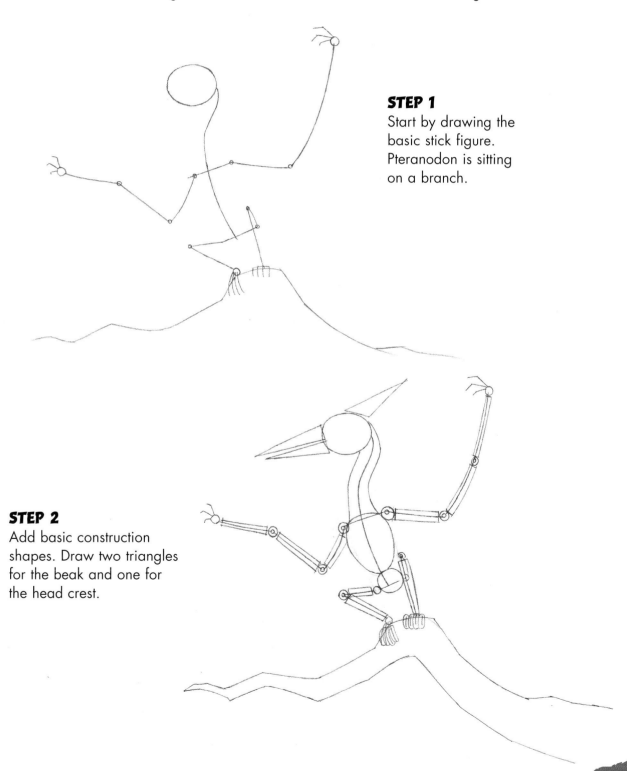

STEP 1

Start by drawing the basic stick figure. Pteranodon is sitting on a branch.

STEP 2

Add basic construction shapes. Draw two triangles for the beak and one for the head crest.

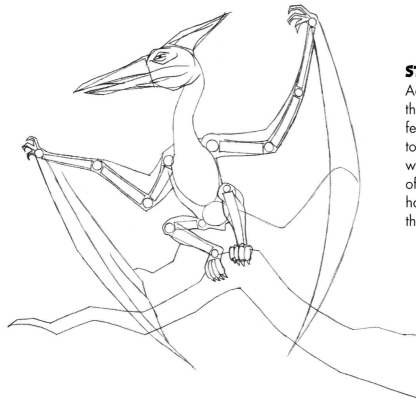

STEP 3

Add skin by drawing around the shapes. Draw the facial features and add definition to the head crest. Draw the wings. They're a continuation of the skin. Notice how they hang like sheets of cloth from the limbs. Add the claws.

STEP 4

Clean up your drawing by erasing your construction shapes. Add detail to the skin and to the tree branch.

STEP 5

Now finalize your pencil drawing. Add lots of detail to the skin, leathery wings, and the branch. Add shading to give your drawing perspective.

STEP 6

Ink over the final
pencil drawing.

DID YOU KNOW?

PTERANODON WAS ABOUT THE SIZE OF A SMALL AIRPLANE, WITH A WINGSPAN THAT MEASURED 33 FEET (10 M) LONG.

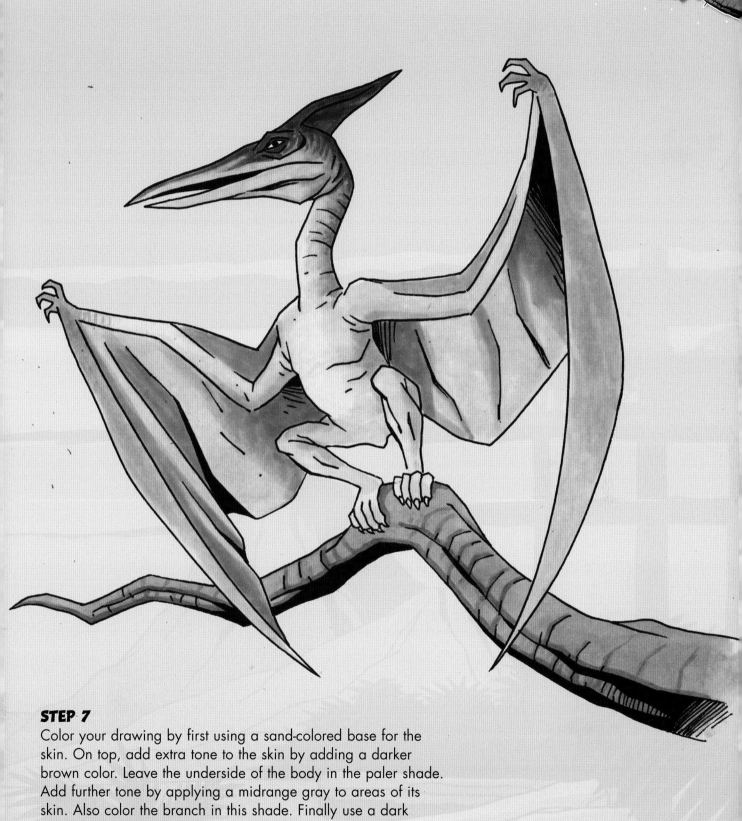

STEP 7

Color your drawing by first using a sand-colored base for the skin. On top, add extra tone to the skin by adding a darker brown color. Leave the underside of the body in the paler shade. Add further tone by applying a midrange gray to areas of its skin. Also color the branch in this shade. Finally use a dark gray to finish off the head and head crest.

ARCHAEOPTERYX

DINO FACT FILE

This small, fascinating creature provides the evolutionary link between dinosaurs and modern-day birds. Archaeopteryx had birdlike features such as the feathers all over its lightweight body and its large brain. Scientists now believe it could fly, not just glide. Its dinosaur features were its sharp teeth, the claws on its wings, and its long bony tail. It was about the size of a crow and ate meat.

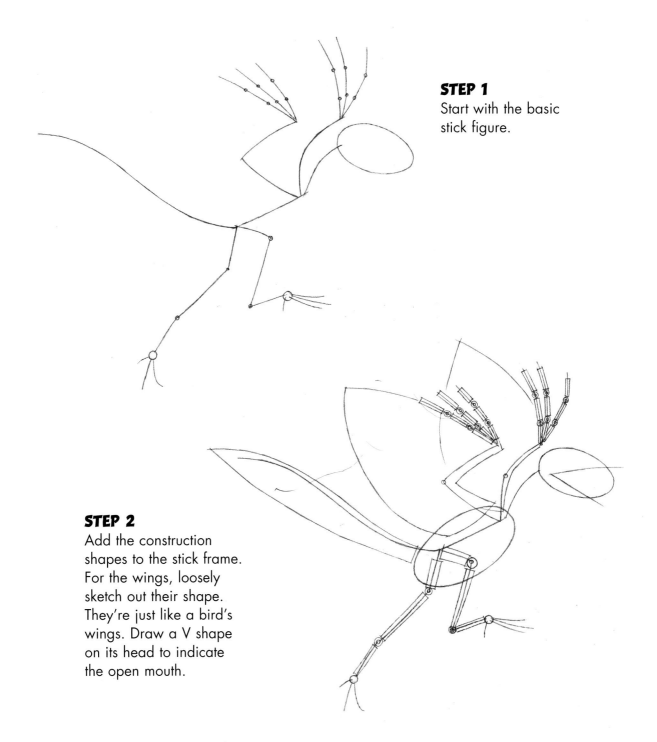

STEP 1
Start with the basic stick figure.

STEP 2
Add the construction shapes to the stick frame. For the wings, loosely sketch out their shape. They're just like a bird's wings. Draw a V shape on its head to indicate the open mouth.

STEP 3
Draw the skin around the construction shapes. Add feathers to the wings, tail, and chest and draw the claws. Add the face, beak, and its open jaw.

STEP 4
Add even more feathers to the wings and the head. Draw its sharp teeth.

STEP 5
Finalize your pencil drawing. Add more details to the legs and face and add lots of line shading to the feathers.

STEP 6
Ink over the finished
pencil drawing.

DID YOU KNOW?
SCIENTISTS DISCOVERED THAT ARCHAEOPTERYX HAD FEATHERS BECAUSE IMPRINTS WERE PRESERVED IN SOFT MUD.

STEP 7

Color the Archaeopteryx starting with a pale yellow for the base of its feathers. Apply lime green over the top, leaving the tips of the feathers yellow. Now add a grass green to the darker areas to create contrast within the feathers. Use sandy colors for the legs and beak and add more yellow to finish the beak and eye.

TROPEOGNATHUS

DINO FACT FILE

Tropeognathus was slightly smaller than Pteranodon, but what it lacked in size, it made up for in razor-sharp teeth. It had a large beak with bony ridges on the top and bottom jaws. It used them to keep balanced as it skimmed along the surface of the water, catching fish to eat. These ridges prevented it from falling in and becoming an easy meal for hungry ocean predators.

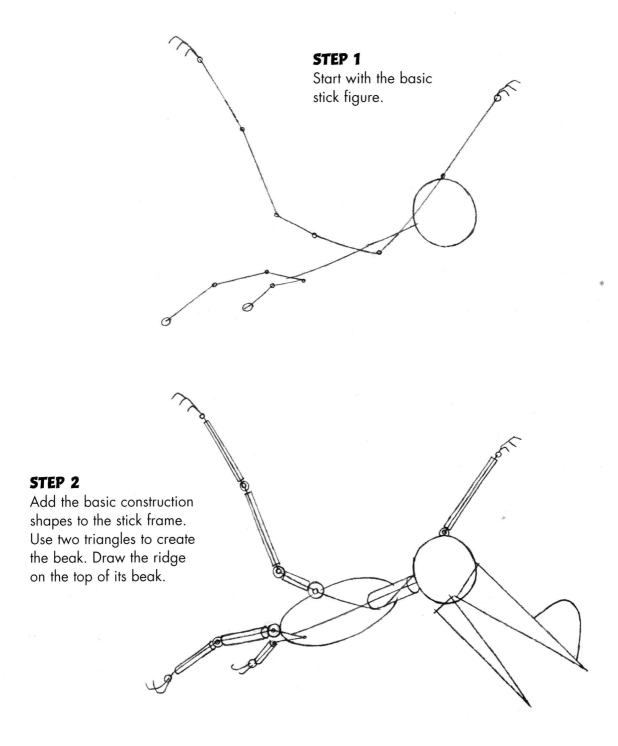

STEP 1
Start with the basic stick figure.

STEP 2
Add the basic construction shapes to the stick frame. Use two triangles to create the beak. Draw the ridge on the top of its beak.

STEP 3

Now add the skin by drawing a line around the shapes. Loosely sketch out the wings. Most wings are wider at the point where they connect to the body and taper into a point at the end. Draw the eyes and facial features.

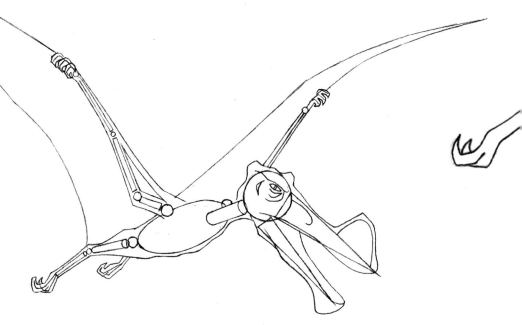

STEP 4

Remove your construction shapes. Add teeth and some detail to the skin and wings.

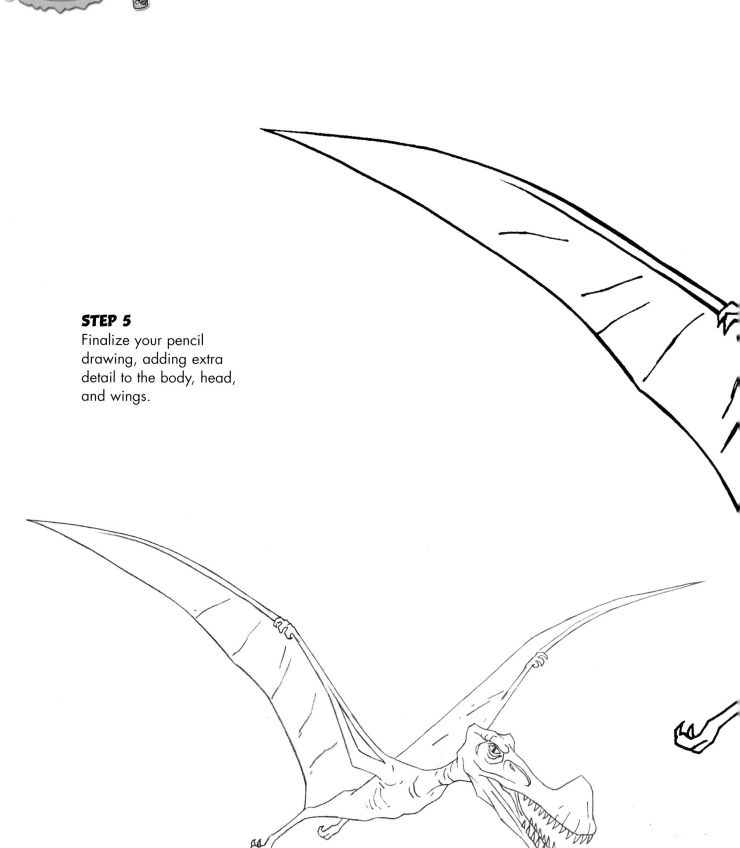

STEP 5
Finalize your pencil drawing, adding extra detail to the body, head, and wings.

STEP 6

Now ink over the pencil lines.
Add shading to the mouth and eye areas.

DID YOU KNOW?

TROPEOGNATHUS WAS ABOUT THE SAME SIZE AS A HANG-GLIDER. ITS WING SPAN MEASURED ABOUT 20 FEET (6 M) IN LENGTH.

STEP 7

Color the drawing starting with a pale sand color for the base. Go over the top of this with pale gray, leaving areas of its belly in the sand color. Apply sky blue over the gray, which will make it look pale blue. Finish off the beak in yellow, the tongue in pink, and the eye in red.

CREATING A SCENE

SKY SCENE FEATURING TROPEOGNATHUS

Tropeognathus could be seen in the sky about 120 million years ago. The Earth was teeming with different species not only on land, but also in the air and the oceans. Flying reptiles were growing to huge sizes and the sea was at its richest. How better to draw this incredible predator than gliding over the ocean, ready to scoop up some fish in its beak.

STEP 1 Draw the horizon line one-third up the page. The perspective lines go farther than the finished drawing does, but it's still useful to draw them in to give you a sense of distance. On the horizon line, draw two sets of mountains. The one on the right will be a volcano. Draw two stick figures that will form the Tropeognathus (see pages 19–25 for the step-by-step guide).

STEP 2 Using the perspective lines as a grid, draw wave shapes going off into the distance. Think of waves like mini mountains to get the shape. Draw swirling lines for the smoke coming from the volcano. Add the construction shapes to Tropeognathus.

STEP 3 Add crests to the waves and detail of movement at the bottom of the waves. Give some definition to the volcano to make it look rocky and finish the smoke. Add some clouds in the sky. Draw the skin, wings, and face of the Tropeognathus.

STEP 4 Complete your final pencil drawing by adding all your shading, which will take the drawing to the next level. Remove any unwanted lines and add your final details.

STEP 5 Color your drawing. Different shades of blue will really bring this seascape to life.

GLOSSARY

cylinders (SIH-len-derz) Shapes with straight sides and circular ends of equal size.

facial (FAY-shul) Of the face.

gouache (GWAHSH) A mixture of nontransparent watercolor paint and gum.

mechanical pencil (mih-KA-nih-kul PENT-sul) A pencil with replaceable lead that may be advanced as needed.

perspective (per-SPEK-tiv) In drawing, changing the relative size and appearance of objects to allow for the effects of distance.

reptiles (REP-tylz) Cold-blooded animals with thin, dry pieces of skin called scales.

sable brushes (SAY-bel BRUSH-ez) Artists' brushes made with the hairs of a sable, a small mammal from northern Asia.

stick figure (STIK FIH-gyur) A simple drawing of a creature with single lines for the head, neck, body, legs, and tail.

tone (TOHN) Any of the possible shades of a particular color.

watercolor (WAH-ter-kuh-ler) Paint made by mixing pigments (substances that give something its color) with water.

INDEX

WEB SITES

Due to the changing nature of Internet links, PowerKids Press has developed an online list of Web sites related to the subject of this book. This site is updated regularly. Please use this link to access the list: www.powerkidslinks.com/ddino/pteranodon/